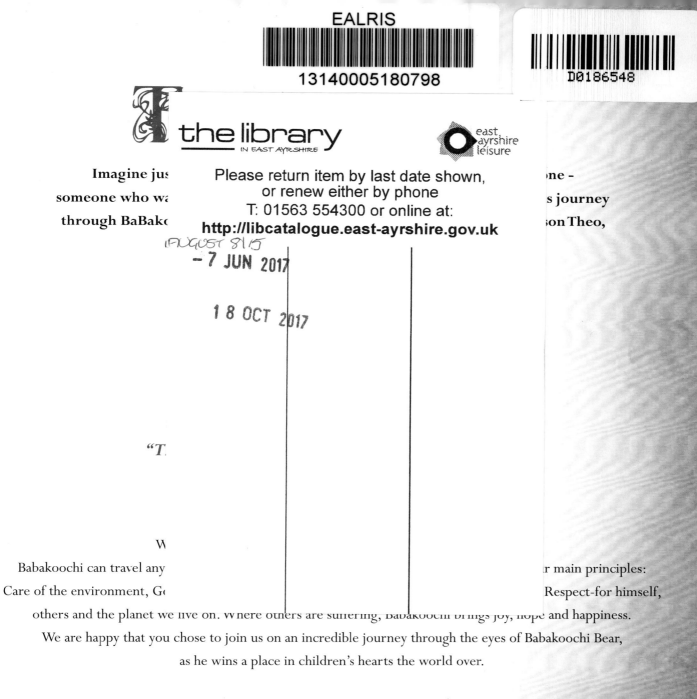

Imagine ju⋯ ⋯ne -
someone who wa⋯ ⋯s journey
through BaBak⋯ ⋯son Theo,

"T⋯

W⋯

Babakoochi can travel any⋯ ⋯r main principles:
Care of the environment, G⋯ ⋯Respect-for himself,
others and the planet we live on. Where others are suffering, Babakoochi brings joy, hope and happiness.
We are happy that you chose to join us on an incredible journey through the eyes of Babakoochi Bear,
as he wins a place in children's hearts the world over.

May Peace Prevail on Earth!

ABOUT THE AUTHOR

Tony Fitzpatrick is best known for his long and illustrious football career. He first came to prominence when Sir Alex Ferguson made him the youngest captain in Scottish Premier League history at the age of just 17. During 18 years at St Mirren FC. His highlight was a Scottish Cup success in 1987. Tony also played for Bristol City and was Youth Director at Livingston FC.

Tony has written many stories in memory of his son, Tony junior, who tragically passed away from acute myeloid leukaemia in 1983 at the tender age of Six. Young Tony's nickname was Babakoochi Bear.

ACKNOWLEDGEMENTS

There are too many to thank. But to name a few...

My late mother Mary and father James for inspiring and supporting me throughout my life and career, and to our artist Graeme Hewitson for advice, friendship and dedication to this project.

Margaret McQueen - my best friend, love you always xxx

For friendship and support: Keith Noble, Darryl Ramage, Garry Brotherston, Paul Falzon, Alex Gollcher, David Wilson, Mark Guidi, Gavin Whyte, Jonny Whyte, Brian Delaney, Ged Malloy, Harry Campbell, Jeff Holmes, Joann Duffy, Melissa Hollywood, Alan Johnston, Joe Livingston, Joe Mc Donagh, Susie & Davie Mark, Bernadette McDade, Rae Patterson, Jim Galsworthy, Simon Farrelly, Raymond Farrelly, Joe Dunn (for poems) Tommy & Elaine Fitzpatrick, Scott & Jackquline Fitzpatrick.

May I also take this opportunity to say a big thank you to Caroline Uchima and all the staff at Allonton House, Dumfriesshire, for their great mission of spreading peace throughout Scotland.

Also to Masahisa Goi, and the Goi Peace Foundation for the common wish of all humanity transcending all boundaries of race, religion and politics, May Peace Prevail On Earth.

Finally to GOSPA, Queen Of Peace, Who said in a message to all of her Children in the World, Let Peace Reign in The Whole World, Which is Without Peace, and longs for Peace.

DEDICATED TO Tony (junior),
Lorraine, Paul, Steven, James & Stephen

This book is also dedicated to Tony's brother Paul who died age 32.

May Peace Prevail on Earth!

INTRODUCTION

There is a tale of magic on the pages of this book.

So find a quiet corner and let's all have a look.

Saber and Theo, are not together anymore.

But little Babakoochi has opened up his door.

With the magic brought by love.

And some help from up above.

A rainbow, some sunshine and some rain.

Keep the Promise, Together Again.

The Promise - Together Again.

Chapter 1:

The winter snow had arrived, covering the vast Freedom Forest and mountain range. The rugged landscape and the river had completely frozen over. In the past twenty four hours the weather had taken a turn for the worse; the temperature had plummeted to thirty degrees below zero. Not since the Big Freeze more than fifty years before had the animals and birds of the Freedom Forest witnessed such wintry conditions. Fortunately everyone had gathered in extra food supplies and sought refuge in their homes, well prepared to sit out the wintry conditions.

However, a month before the Big Freeze, Sabre - the great white bear - had arrived with his fierce army of rebels to seek out and destroy all who lived in Freedom Forest and in the mountains. Tensions were running high and all the animals were frightened for their lives. Sabre had arrived with anger and revenge in his heart. He was in such a rage that he had turned against the Supreme Life Force and had sworn vengeance against all life on Mother Earth.

Sabre carried such bitterness in his heart because his only son, Theo, the young bear cub had passed away into the Long Sleep after a short illness and had passed over to the World of Light and Understanding. No one could console the great white bear.

Now, with his army in position, Sabre was ready to unleash his rage upon all the animals of Freedom Lands as soon as the weather cleared, especially against Koocha their wise and brave leader who had come to confront Sabre. Sabre had drawn out his mighty sword and had it pressed against Koocha's chest, preparing to run the cold steel blade into the brave leader's heart. The animals gathered behind their leader gasped with fear at the sight of Sabre poised ready to take Koocha's life!

Just then the great white bear noticed a small cub running towards them. The brave young cub was called Babakoochi. He had broken free from his mother's grasp on seeing what Sabre was about to do to his father and leader, Koocha. The young cub, showing no signs of fear or concern for his own life, made straight for the spot where Sabre stood with his sword pressed up against his father's heart. Babakoochi stood by Koocha's side, refusing to move. The young bear was willing to give up his own life for his father and the other animals.

Silence fell over the land - not a sound could be heard. It was as if time stood still.

All the animals waited to see what the great white bear would do next. At that point something changed deep inside Sabre's heart. To everyone's amazement the great white bear threw down his sword, took a few steps back and bowed his head in respect for the courage and bravery shown - in the face of death - by Koocha and Babakoochi. Sabre immediately vowed to try to mend his evil ways!

Before leaving with his fierce band, Sabre told Koocha that his son Theo had been a brave young bear and that he would have done the same thing -- been willing to give up his life for others. Just before he passed, Sabre had whispered a promise to his son, "Together again", but Sabre didn't know if this would ever happen and all he felt now was anger.

In spite of this, Sabre was so inspired by Babakoochi's actions that he presented a great gift to the young cub. The gift was the magic Peace Pole which had been given to Sabre many years before by the Supreme Life Force, to spread peace and harmony to all who lived on Mother Earth.

Sabre admitted, with great sadness, that after the passing of his son Theo he had used the powers of the Peace Pole to bring fear and unrest throughout the lands. Now he felt in his heart that Theo would have been pleased that he had given the magic Peace Pole to Babakoochi so that it could be used for its true purpose - to bring peace and harmony to all. When the time was right, Babakoochi would be told how to use the Peace Pole.

Chapter 2

After Sabre and his band left, a blizzard came howling down from the mountain and roared through the forest making ghostly howling noises as it passed by Babakoochi's family's cave.

Inside the cave it was warm and cosy and Babakoochi and his little sister Poppy had been allowed to stay up later than usual to listen to Suman, their wise old grandfather, reading them a story from the book "Tales of Truth." The young bear cubs loved stories and Suman had told them about David Livingstone, a humble man who was a great explorer and had travelled to a land called Africa to take the message of the Supreme Life Force to that country.

Old Grey Bear, a great story-teller who often came to visit and share his wonderful adventures with the animals and birds of Freedom Forest, had told them in one of his tales how he had even met David Livingstone and helped him on his quest to spread the message. When Suman had finished the story, the young cubs' mother, Chie reminded them to brush their teeth before getting into bed, and also to say their prayers. She asked them specially to say a prayer for all their loved ones who had passed over to the World of Light and Understanding.

Koocha and Suman sat down by the big log fire and resumed their game of chess - a game the two bears loved to play against each other. Suman, who had been taught from an early age by the wise bears of the mountains, had been the champion of all Freedom Lands for many years and now his son Koocha was almost as good.

Poppy was soon snuggled up in bed and Babakoochi went to brush his teeth. Up and down - not from side to side. He was using his toothbrush the way his mother had shown him. He HATED cleaning his teeth.

He thought to himself, "It is so boring brushing your teeth." Then he remembered a song Mrs Rose his school teacher had taught him and his classmates to sing when they brushed their teeth. Mrs Rose told them to use their inner voice to sing or all the toothpaste would spill out of their mouths and make an almighty mess.

Babakoochi started to sing, "This is the way you brush your teeth, brush your teeth, brush your teeth. This is the way you brush your teeth on a cold and frosty morning!" The young bear let out a loud laugh when he saw his reflection in the mirror - his mouth and chin were covered in white toothpaste! He then started to make funny faces, opening up his mouth and growling, baring his teeth full of toothpaste.

He thought to himself, "I look like a wild wolf foaming at the mouth." He found this so funny he was laughing out very loudly. Chie, his mother, heard his laughter and called to him, "Babakoochi! Time for bed. Stop carrying on or you will wake up Poppy. It's very late and you will find it hard to get up in the morning." Babakoochi shouted down that he was sorry and made his way to the side of his bed where he knelt down to say his prayers. Prayers finished, the young bear slipped under his blankets and snuggled down.

As he lay there staring up at the roof of the cave, he thought how lucky he was to be safely tucked up in his warm comfy bed on such a cold winter's evening like this. The young bear could hear the mountain wolves calling to each other in the distance. Normally the howling, chilling sounds the wolves made would have sent cold shivers down the young bear's spine, but tonight he felt safe and secure in his bed, far away from hungry wolves.

Babakoochi was finding it difficult to get to sleep; his mind was too active. He tried a trick his grandfather Suman had told him to try if he could not sleep. He started to count sheep - one, two, three... Then Babakoochi's attention was taken by the sound of the branches of the trees outside bending and thrashing about in the strong wind. The young bear was getting scared so he put on his lamp and up in a corner he saw one of his friends - Stegs the spider, who was weaving his web trying to make it strong enough to catch flies but the wind coming in was shaking the web and making Stegs' work very difficult. Babakoochi watched the big spider working and marvelled at the way his friend could hang upside down from the roof of the cave with just his web to take his weight.

As he watched his friend Babakoochi's eyes became heavy. The young bear let out a loud yawn - AAAAAAH. He tried to keep his eyes open but the more he tried to fight off sleep the heavier his eyes became and he soon fell into a deep sleep.

Chapter 3

As Babakoochi slept, a bright light appeared above his bed lighting up the cave. Babakoochi woke to hear a gentle voice speaking to him. It was the voice of the Supreme Life Force. The voice told him that the Peace Pole that Sabre had given him had magical, mystical powers. When the time was right, Babakoochi would be able to use it to bring the people and animals from this world to meet up again with lost loved ones who had passed over to the World of Light and Understanding.

A chance for loved ones to meet at their favourite meeting place and to share in the times of fun and joy they had when they were together on Mother Earth. The bright light grew stronger and the gentle voice continued speaking, but now with great sadness in its tone.

"Babakoochi, it makes my heart grow sad to watch so many of my children not taking the time and opportunity to tell their loved ones every day that they love and care for them. How foolish they are, locking away these beautiful emotions and feelings deep inside their hearts! The great enemy, fear and its sister rejection hold so many back from sharing those wonderful words 'I love you.' Too many carry the regrets for the rest of their lives for not being able to say and share those magical words with each other. Babakoochi, I have listened to my children's cries and I have chosen you to be their guide. I will give you the power to take loved ones from each world to walk through the rainbow and meet up again. When you plant the Peace Pole in the ground beside you and say the words, 'May peace prevail on earth,' a rainbow will appear on top of the Peace Pole and it will create a colourful gateway for you and those who have been chosen to meet up with their loved ones."

The bright light then started to fade away until it was completely gone.
When Babakoochi awoke it was morning. Daylight was streaming into the cave.

He rubbed his eyes and then rubbed his nose; it felt so itchy. The young bear let out a long yawn, stretched his arms over his head and pushed his legs down towards the bottom of his bed. He felt the coldness of the wood against the soles of his feet. OOOOOOH ! The young bear quickly pulled his feet back up under the warm blankets. He checked to see if his friend Stegs the spider was still up in the corner of the cave. He was still entangled in his web fast asleep.

Babakoochi sat up in his bed, tried to wipe away the sleep from his eyes and looked around the room. "That's strange - no light," he thought. "I must have been dreaming!" He got up out of bed and walked over towards the front of the cave. He noticed the wind had dropped and only a gentle breeze blew through the Forest although it was still snowing heavily. Babakoochi looked across to the mountain ranges but they were barely visible; dark black snow clouds hung over them like a thick blanket. He could not see the summits of the vast mountains. He turned his attention down towards the forest. Thick white snow covered the whole landscape, the trees and bushes were mostly hidden under the thick snow and not even a footprint could be seen on the forest floor. The young bear stood for a few minutes watching the large snowflakes floating past. He loved to watch the snow falling. Maybe he and his family could go out and play in the snow later.

Babakoochi checked his tongue in the mirror; it was nice and pink looking. His mother told him that meant he was healthy. He washed his face and howled – the water was freezing. He brushed his teeth but this time without singing his song then he went to join his family for breakfast. He sniffed the air and a big smile broke across his face. He had picked up the smell of his favourite breakfast - hot honey cakes! Chie was cooking breakfast for the family.

"Good morning, Babakoochi!" they all shouted out to him. "Good morning!" the young bear answered back, yawning at the same time. "Did you sleep well, Babakoochi?" Chie enquired. "Yes mother, like a wooden log."

Chie smiled at her son and told him to sit down for his breakfast with the rest of the family.

"I have made your favourites - hot honey cakes - this morning, but first a bowl of hot porridge."

Koocha, his father joked, "You better hurry, Son. Your sister Poppy is very hungry this morning and will have all the honey cakes eaten before you get any."

Chie interrupted, "Don't listen to your father. There is plenty for everyone."

Chie turned to Koocha and said, "Stop teasing him! You know how much he loves his honey cakes."

Suman, Babakoochi's wise old grandfather, had noticed his grandson was being very quiet and not his usual self. He seemed lost in a daydream and he was staring into space.

"Is everything all right?" Suman asked. "Is there something troubling you? Have you something on your mind this morning?" Babakoochi stayed silent for a moment, and then he shared what had happened during the night. Chie walked across and gave her son a hug.

"You have been given a great blessing. The Supreme Life Force has chosen you to do this wonderful thing."

Koocha interrupted and asked Babakoochi if he knew when he would be going on his quest.

"No, Father, but the voice said it would be soon." Suman said, "The Supreme Life Force works in mysterious ways. I am sure all will be revealed in good time."

Chie placed a bowl of hot porridge in front of her son and said, "Eat up, Babakoochi. You will need all your strength and energy to go on these journeys." Then she turned to the rest of the family and told them not to ask any more questions and let Babakoochi enjoy his breakfast before it got cold. There would be plenty of time later to ask more questions.

After breakfast Koocha and Suman resumed their game of chess from the night before. Babakoochi and Poppy played in the snow and later Chie read Babakoochi and Poppy another story from the Sacred Book.

Later that evening the family all agreed to give Babakoochi their blessings and support, to help him prepare for his journeys ahead. The snow had stopped falling outside; there was now just a gentle breeze blowing through the forest.

16

Chapter 4

The next morning Babakoochi asked his mother's permission to go down to the frozen lake and watch the animals skating across the ice. Chie agreed on one condition: he did not go onto the ice himself. Over the last few winters a few of the young animals had fallen through the thin ice and drowned. He promised he would only watch from his favourite rock beside the lake. He gave his mother a big hug and made his way down through the forest.

The snow was very deep and the ground was very slippery in places. The young bear would have to be very careful where he stepped; it could be dangerous. He continued carefully through a grove of silver birch trees that were leaning over with the weight of the heavy snow on their branches.

When Babakoochi met his friend Benny the badger, he and his brothers were busy building a snowman. Benny shouted to Babakoochi to come and join them and help them build the snowman. The young bear was excited and loved playing in the snow, so he joined in. Then Benny bent down, filled up his paws with snow and made it into a giant snowball, took aim and threw it straight at Babakoochi. The big snowball hit the young bear right on the back of his head , it exploded into pieces, the cold wet snow ran down his neck and he let out a loud howl. "Aaaaaaaah! That's freezing.

 Benny shouted, "Out strike one!" His brothers fell about with laughter and shouted, "Great shot, Benny!" Babakoochi joined in the snowball fight. He gave as good as he got, hitting Benny with a direct hit right on the young badger's face. They were all having so much fun playing in the snow but Babakoochi wanted to go down to the lake to watch the animals skating. He said his farewells to Benny and his brothers and thanked them for letting him help build the snowman.

When Babakoochi arrived at the frozen lake he sat down on his favourite rock where he had a great view of everything that was happening on the ice. He soon spotted two of his school friends, Brooke and Barry - two bear cubs - trying to keep their balance on the slippery ice. Babakoochi burst out laughing when Brooke and Barry went crashing down on their bottoms on the hard ice. He yelled over, "Hope you enjoyed your trip!" Even the two young bears saw the funny side of his joke and started to laugh.

Babakoochi's attention was soon drawn to the beautiful rugged mountain range that surrounded Freedom Forest. He looked high above the peaks. The sky was now clear with not a storm cloud in sight, but it was Aquila the golden eagle that had taken his attention. He watched her soaring over the mountain tops using the strong thermals to glide with ease across the sky. Then Aquila would hover and fold her massive wings in close to her body, retract her powerful talons and dive at great speeds towards the rugged landscape. She looked like a missile heading for its target; then just before making contact with the ground Aquila would open up her mighty wings and swoop back up into the sky. Babakoochi watched in awe at the flying skills of Aquila. He wished he could fly! What fun it must be to be able to soar high above the mountains.

Then a strong feeling of love came over the young bear's heart as he heard once again the voice from the night before; The voice of the Supreme Life Force. "Babakoochi," it said, "It is time for you to go on a journey. Go to Sabre the great white bear. He is in great despair and needs help. Take him through the rainbow to meet up with his son Theo again. Go soon! Time is of the essence."

Babakoochi hurried home to tell his family that it was time for him to go on his journey. His family felt so proud that their son had been chosen for this wonderful quest. The time had come! They walked out into the garden which was still covered in deep snow. Babakoochi took a few steps forward then planted

the Peace Pole down through the snow into the ground and said, "May peace prevail on earth."

Immediately strong vibrations came from the pole, then, by magic, a fountain of bright colours came flowing out of the top of the Peace Pole. The colours started to mix together making a beautiful rainbow that arched over the garden. Poppy shouted out in excitement, "Look mother; a rainbow!" Chie bent down and picked her daughter up in her arms.

19

MAY
PEACE

PREVAIL
ON

EARTH

"Yes Poppy. It is such a wonderful sight. I love rainbows too. They bring back memories of when I was a young cub like you. I would stand with my mother looking over the mountains and river watching the rainbows arch over our lands. My mother used to say that many people would tell you that you would find a pot of gold at the end of a rainbow but our wise bears of Freedom Mountain believe differently. They say when you walk through a rainbow it will lead you to your loved ones who have passed over to the World of Light and Understanding. It is also our connection to the Supreme Life Force. He sends rainbows to remind us that human beings, animals, in fact all life forces on Mother Earth are connected. We are all brothers and sisters - we are all one.

Chapter 5

Babakoochi waved goodbye to his family and walked into the tunnel of colours. He felt no fear walking through the colourful gateway; in fact just the opposite: he felt very calm and peaceful inside. He looked all around him. Beautiful colours swirled round; children's singing voices echoed around him; vibrations started coming through the pole again - Wooooooooosh! The colours all began making their way into the top of the Peace Pole again and all of a sudden Babakoochi found himself standing in a meadow at the edge of a small stream.

The young bear looked around him. Tall, lush grass was swaying from side to side in the gentle breeze blowing through the meadow. He noticed that the trees at the edge of the meadow were much bigger than back home. In the opposite direction fields of beautiful flowers covered the landscape as far as the eye could see. Babakoochi sniffed the stream running through the meadow. The water was fresh. His nose picked up the scent of pine trees. He listened carefully. The sounds coming out of the forest reminded him of home, but his instincts told him something was different about this land.

Looking down into the clear water of the stream he saw big fish, small fish, all different colours, swimming past. He saw his reflection in the water and got caught up in his thoughts for a moment. All of a sudden a big silver fish leapt out of the water and landed back in the stream near to where Babakoochi was standing. As the large fish entered the water it made such a splash that it showering

MAY
PEACE

PREVAIL
ON

EARTH

cold water all over the poor young bear. He was drenched; soaked through to the skin. He was shaking himself, trying to clear the cold water off his fur when he heard loud laughter coming from below him in the stream.

"The big silver one is called a Fish of Fortune," a croaky voice shouted up at him. Babakoochi looked down and to his surprise he saw a giant frog sitting on a large rock at the side of the riverbank. And the frog was smiling back at him!

"A Fish of Fortune?" The young bear asked, looking bewildered.

"Yes, my young furry friend. But don't worry. You will come to understand all in good time." The frog laughed out loud. Babakoochi introduced himself.

"Pleased to meet you; I am Fatso the frog. I am called after my grandfather. In fact my family is full of Fatsos," the big frog said proudly. Babakoochi tried to hold in his laughter but when he thought what the name of the frog was he could not hold in his laughter any longer.

"Babakoochi, what's so funny?" the big frog enquired.

"Oh sorry, Fatso," the young bear put his paw up to his mouth trying to disguise his laughter. "When you said your family was full of Fatsos it made me laugh."

The big frog looked up at the young bear and said, "I don't understand. What's so funny about being called Fatso?"

Babakoochi felt ashamed as he told the big frog that back where he came from the name Fatso would be used against him, and he would be made fun of by all the humans and animals. The name Fatso was used for overweight and obese people and animals.

MAY
PEACE

PREVAIL
ON

EARTH

The big frog shook his head. "They should be ashamed of themselves. There is a name for them - Bullies! Many years ago we had such people who lived here in our land but they were asked to leave. No one would put up with this bad behaviour. Bullying will not be tolerated in this land."

Babakoochi said he was so sorry for laughing and had learned a lesson; that he was just as much to blame as the bullies because his laughter could encourage them to carry on making fun of others.

Fatso said, "I am glad you have learned this lesson. I hope you take it back home with you and in the future help all the children and adults who are suffering through being bullied." Babakoochi promised he would and then asked his new friend if he had seen Sabre, the great white bear. Fatso smiled and pointed across the stream to a clump of trees.

"There he is sitting under the trees," the frog whispered. "Sabre has been sitting there for days all by himself, not speaking to anyone. He has been very upset. I am afraid he has been missing his son, Theo and is finding life very difficult to cope with without him. We are all so worried about our big friend. He has shut himself away from the world.

Babakoochi smiled, "Yes I think you are right, my friend. He is hurting so much but I have been sent by the Supreme Life Force to help him with his sad loss."

"How can you do this?" Fatso asked.

Babakoochi laughed. "As you said earlier to me, Fatso; all will be revealed, all in good time!" The two friends laughed out loud and said their goodbyes

25

Babakoochi made his way across the stream. The water was very cold but it felt very refreshing on the young bear's feet. He was now standing beside the great white bear and he spoke softly to him but there was no response.

"Sabre it's me - Babakoochi. I have been sent by the Supreme Life Force to take you to see your son Theo again." Sabre stirred and took his massive paws slowly away from his face and looked at Babakoochi. "It is you! I can't believe my eyes. I thought I was hearing things."
Babakoochi smiled, "Yes it is me, my big friend. I am here to take you through the rainbow to meet up and spend time with Theo again." Sabre looked up in confusion.

"Sorry, I have not been thinking straight these past few days, but did I hear you right? I can meet up with my son again. How can this be?" he asked.

Babakoochi explained about how the Peace Pole Sabre had given him could now be used to bring lost loved ones from each world to meet up again at their favourite places. They could spend time together sharing the fun things they did together when both lived on Mother Earth. The Supreme Life Force had seen how much his children were suffering through the loss of their loved ones and had heard their cries for help.

"You my dear friend are the first to go through to meet your loved one," the young bear said. He asked Sabre to follow him. The big bear got up off the lush grass and stood beside his little friend.

"For weeks now I have felt Theo's energy around me," Sabre said. "Sometimes I can still pick up his scent. All my instincts tell me he is close by. One day I could have sworn I saw his reflection in the river, but when I checked the water again he was gone."

Babakoochi interrupted his big friend. "My mother always says that we must learn to open our minds and hearts to what our instincts are telling us. When my grandmother passed over to the Land of Light and Understanding she told my mother just days before, that death was nothing at all. 'I have only slipped into the next room. I am I, and you are you. Whatever we were to each other, we still are.'"

With tears in his eyes Sabre thanked his young friend.

"The words you speak give me great comfort in my heart," he said.

Babakoochi walked a few steps forward, planted the Peace Pole in the ground beside him and said, "May peace prevail on earth."

Wooooooooooosh! Once again a multi coloured fountain shot out of the top of the Peace Pole and formed a rainbow over them. The young bear took Sabre's hand and guided him into the gateway of colours.

Soon the sound of children singing echoed all around them; different bright colours swirled round and round. It felt so peaceful. Babakoochi then asked Sabre to think of his favourite place where he would like to meet up again with his son Theo.

"That is easy, my young friend." A huge smile appeared across Sabre's face. "The happiest times Theo and I spent together were in the Magic Forest!"

The words had hardly left the big bear's mouth when all of a sudden they were standing in the Magic Forest. Sabre looked around in amazement.

"This is the place," he said. "Look over there by that big oak tree. That's where Theo and I spent hours playing." Babakoochi could hardly contain himself. He smiled up at Sabre so pleased to see his friend happy.

"Go Sabre, and sit under the tree and think about Theo and the good times spent there together."

The big white bear made his way towards the tree. He sat down under its spreading branches and leant against its trunk. The cold wood felt good against his fur and he couldn't resist rubbing his back up and down on the rough bark. Aaaaaaaaah ! That felt so good.

Sabre relaxed and closed his eyes. He listened to the beautiful sounds of nature around him. In the distance a woodpecker was busy knocking his large beak against the trunk of a tree. He could hear the sound of running water nearby and the birds singing their songs. He loved just sitting, watching and listening to all the creatures going about their daily work.

He felt so relaxed now that he began to think about Theo and the times he and his son had spent playing on the old rope swing. It had been so much fun.   A thought suddenly came into Sabre's mind; of course, the swing! He opened his eyes and quickly got to his feet. He wondered if the old rope swing would still be there. He looked about to ask Babakoochi but his young friend had gone. He checked and looked all around but he was nowhere to be seen. Sabre walked slowly round to the other side of the big oak tree and to his great delight saw the old swing still hanging from the branches of the big tree.

It was a very hot day in the Magic Forest but a gentle breeze blew through the trees cooling the big bear. He sniffed around him and noticed a beautiful scent filling the air. He wondered what the wonderful smell was that had the fragrance of flowers but also something quite different.   He sniffed the air again - the scent was becoming stronger. What was that beautiful smell? His nose followed the fragrance down to a field of thick, long grass. The strange thing was that there were no flowers in the field, so where was the beautiful scent coming from?

Suddenly Sabre saw movement in the tall grass. Something was making its way towards him. Then a voice was calling out. The big bear knew that sound: it was his son Theo's voice, "Dad! Dad! It's me, Theo."

Chapter 7

The big bear sank down on his knees when he saw Theo coming out of the tall grass right in front of him. He opened his arms and Theo ran straight into them. He held his son in close to his powerful chest and gave him a mighty hug. It felt wonderful to feel his son in his arms again. Sabre could feel the tears streaming down his face.

"Oh, Theo, I have missed you so much!"
"I have missed you too Dad, and I love you so much."

The big bear got to his feet still holding Theo in his arms and began to dance with his son. He then threw Theo up in the air and caught him on the way back down - something Sabre had always done to Theo since he was a very young cub. Theo had always loved this game with his father.

"Theo, the old swing is still hanging on the oak tree. Do you want to go and play on it?"
"Oh yes, Dad," Theo's face lit up. "I love playing on that swing."

Theo climbed up onto the swing and Sabre pushed him higher and higher.
"Look, Dad. I am an eagle soaring high; I am an angel passing by. Wheeeeeeeee! Wheeeeeeeee!" he called out.

Sabre could see the joy on his son's face; it was just like old times. They were having so much fun together and they played for hours.

Then Theo asked his father if they could go down to the Magic River and catch the silver Fish of Fortune. This was something Sabre and Theo had done every day together. The Fish of Fortune was very special because when caught it would then spit out a silver pearl from its mouth to the one who had captured it in his hands. Inside each beautiful pearl was a small scroll with a message of hope written on it. Sabre smiled and agreed.

Theo took off and ran as fast as he could towards the river.
"Last one in the river is a big, soft, fluffy teddy bear!" he shouted back.

Sabre laughed out loud, and then made a dash to try and catch up with his son who had given himself a head start. Father and son dived into the water together, Theo heading straight to the bottom. He swam down as fast as he could because he knew the silver Fish of Fortune loved swimming on the river bed where they could hide themselves among the shiny rocks but Theo had spotted one swimming just above a big boulder. He gave chase but the silver fish were very fast swimmers and slippery customers and very hard to catch.

Theo was just about to grab the big fish when it twisted away, spinning round in a different direction. Theo was not going to give up that easily. He turned around and gave chase again and this time he managed to lunge out and grab the fish by its tail. It tried to slip out of his grip but the young bear hung on to the fish's tail with all his strength…… He had caught a Fish of Fortune!

Theo headed straight for the surface clutching the big silver fish in his paws.
"Well done, Theo! Great catch." Sabre cried out and without saying another word he dived straight down into the water and in a short time he surfaced holding onto another big silver fish.

"Can I get my pearl out first?" Theo asked and of course Sabre agreed. Theo rubbed the fish's belly and it spat the silver pearl out into his paw. Theo then let his fish go free back into the river. Sabre repeated what his son had done; his fish spat out a pearl into his giant paws, and he let his fish go free back into the river too.

Now father and son each had a glistening silver pearl and they made their way out of the river to sit side by side on the grassy bank where they dried off in the scorching sun. Theo tried to open his pearl first. He fumbled about, twisting and turning it but it was so difficult to open up. Sabre was laughing as he watched his son trying to open the pearl.

"Theo, just pull it open. Don't turn it," he said.

Theo did as his father said. Success! The pearl opened up and Theo took out the small scroll of paper, unrolled it, and read aloud to Sabre.

"Death is not the end of life, and my spirit will never leave you." The big white bear's eyes filled up with tears.
"Son that is such a beautiful message."
 Sabre then opened up his pearl and read out the message.
"Don't let your heart be troubled. Put your trust in me. If you believe in me, then anything is possible."

Theo smiled at his father and said he had heard the Supreme Life Force use these words many times. Sabre looked down at his son with great pride and thought how much he had grown up. Father and son lay back down on the thick soft grass, enjoying the peace and the sunshine. They felt so content just lying in each other's company.

After a short time resting, Sabre asked Theo if he was hungry and he replied that he was starving. Sabre suggested they go to their friends the honey bees and ask them for some fresh honey. Theo was delighted - he loved the taste of fresh honey. They made their way down by the trees, laughing and joking and telling stories about the good times they had spent together when Theo was still on Mother Earth. Suddenly they were interrupted by a swarm of bees flying by.

"We must be close to the hives." said Sabre. "That was a group of worker bees that just flew past."
"Yes Dad. Listen, I can hear the bees making buzzing sounds."
"Look over there Theo," Sabre interrupted his son, "beside the cedar trees. It's the bee hives."

Just then some young honey bees flew to greet them. "Good afternoon," buzzed the bees. "Would you like some fresh honey to eat? It was made fresh this morning." "Oh yes please," said Theo, already licking his lips with his tongue at the thought of the taste of the sweet honey.

The young bees led them over to the bee hives. They told father and son to help themselves to as much honey as they could eat. Sabre reached up and broke a few twigs off the branches of a tree, then placed the thin pieces of wood into the honeycombs and began to twirl them around in the thick sweet honey.

"My favourites, honey pop sticks." Theo shouted out in excitement. The young bear was now enjoying licking the fresh honey off the stick. Sabre started to laugh watching his son whose lips and chin were now covered in honey.

Just then Beatrice the queen bee flew over to speak to them.
"Oh I am so pleased to see that you are enjoying the fresh honey, and it fills my heart with great joy to see both of you back together again. We all miss your visits and your company."

Sabre and Theo thanked the queen bee for the bees' generosity in sharing their hard earned supplies of honey with them. Beatrice then spoke of her concern about how the humans had become so selfish and greedy in their ways against Mother Nature, taking far more than they needed, cutting down rainforests and polluting the air and the rivers and oceans.

The queen bee let out a deep sigh. "It is only a matter of time until the damage the humans are causing on Mother Earth won't be able to be reversed. Don't they understand they are putting us all at risk and their children's children? What chance do they have if this destruction continues at the rate it is now? I'm sorry..... I just get so angry and despair at the way the humans are treating our beautiful planet."

Sabre agreed with what Beatrice had to say but told her there was now great hope, and things could change. He explained about Babakoochi and the great gift bestowed upon him by the Supreme Life Force. He told Beatrice that the young bear had been given magical powers to guide children and young animals through the rainbow, to try and change the mind-set of adults towards their environment and to all other life forces living on Mother Earth. Sabre also explained the great gift Babakoochi was given to reunite loved ones from both worlds to meet up again, and that he had been guided through the rainbow to be with his son Theo again.

"This is wonderful news!" Beatrice said. "It gives me joy and hope in my heart to hear of such things. I hope maybe one day soon I can meet up with this young bear and perhaps help him in his quest to change the world."

"That day may come sooner than you think, Beatrice," Sabre said, smiling.

It was now time for the two bears to leave the honey bees to continue the hard work of making more honey. They said their goodbyes to Beatrice and made their way back through the forest. It was becoming even hotter now and they were feeling very uncomfortable in their thick fur.
"Dad, I feel too hot," Theo said, slowing down.
"Follow me, Son. I have a surprise for you." Sabre replied and strode on.

The young bear trudged behind his father finding it hard to keep up. The sun was beating down and the heat was becoming unbearable. Everywhere they looked the animals and birds had taken shelter from the scorching sun.

The big bear pushed through some thick bushes and entered a dark tunnel. Then, to Theo's delight, as they came out the other end of the tunnel they were greeted by a massive wall of falling water. Theo knew exactly where they had come out. It was a magical place the animals and birds had named 'The Edge of the World.' A giant waterfall came tumbling down from high cliffs and the sunlight shining on the spray cast shimmering rainbows in the air.

Sabre signalled to his son to come and stand under the waterfall with him as, according to their traditions, bears had always done. It was believed by the wise Council of Bears that if you stood under the waterfall just before sunrise the water would wash away all the troubles of the day. Also, as the sun slowly rose in the sky for the start of a new day, the water would cleanse your mind, body, and spirit. The wise bears believed that the early part of the morning had magical, mystical powers.

Sabre and Theo stood under the freezing water which took their breath away but also refreshed their hot skin and fur, after being out in the hot sun all day. Feeling much better they made their way out of the waterfall and sat up on the grass, well away from the cold sprays of water bouncing up from the giant rocks below. Father and son lay back on the soft sweet grass which felt so soft against their wet fur and let the sun dry them.

They stayed silent for a few minutes listening to the crickets chirping all around them. A cool breeze had started to blow through the Magic Forest and it was a welcome relief from the hot sun. It also rustled through the leaves make a gentle, peaceful sound. A honey bee buzzed by Theo's ear but he felt too relaxed to let it bother him.

A red admiral butterfly landed right on Sabre's wet nose making his nose feel itchy. The big bear did not want to use his giant paws to remove the butterfly in case he hurt it, so he blew as hard as he could trying to get the butterfly to move away. After a few strong gusts the butterfly finally moved off his nose and flew to a nearby flower. Theo had been watching his father struggle to get the butterfly to move. He found it so funny!

"Dad, you sounded like a giant whale that swims in the ocean," he laughed, 'puffing and snorting, trying to move that butterfly.' Sabre told Theo how much he missed him and felt helpless, and was full of guilt for not being able to save his son's life from the rare virus. "If only I had spotted your illness earlier maybe I could have saved you, Theo."

The young bear looked up lovingly into his father's eyes. "No, dad. There was nothing more you could have done. My journey on earth was always meant to be a short one. It was my time to go. I was needed in the World of Light and Understanding."

"What was it like at the moment of your passing over?" Sabre asked. Theo gathered his thoughts for a moment before answering his father. "I remember lying in my bed. The pain running through my body was unbearable. Then above me I saw a tunnel of bright colours swirling around, and my spirit left my body. The closer I got to the swirling colours the more my pain disappeared. When I went into the rainbow tunnel all my pain had gone leaving a feeling of peace. I felt very calm with no fear. Up ahead a brilliant light shone and I just knew to head for it.

When I got to the light I passed through into a wonderful garden. I noticed a beautiful scent all around me like the wild flowers of our forest. But there were no flowers, just grasslands as far as the eye could see. In the distance I could make out the shapes of humans and animals but as I got closer I noticed a difference; the shapes weren't like bodies on Mother Earth. These were just pure light.

I realised that I had great understanding; not only about the place I had found myself in, but also about life on earth. Everything was very clear to me: I had an understanding of Life itself."

"The tunnel of bright swirling colours you spoke of sounds very much like how I got here to meet up with you. Are you happy in your new home?" Sabre asked his son.

"Yes Dad. I'm happier now than I have ever been. I live in a place that has no illness, no fear, or worry. While we are on Mother Earth, we must live with illness, fear and worry in order to progress into the World of Light and Understanding.

Living in the physical world is like walking a thousand miles in uncomfortable shoes; when you take the uncomfortable shoes off the relief is incredible. Just like when you leave the physical body, the relief is the same.

Dad, I know you miss my physical body but if you open up your mind and feelings you will feel the energy of my love all around you. I can feel your energy coming from your spirit.

In the World of Light and Understanding we can understand our true thoughts and feelings. During any circumstance you face, Dad, you can communicate with me at any time. I am free to travel anywhere in the universe."

"Is that why sometimes I can feel your love around me?"

"Of course it is. Always put your trust in your instincts and feelings when you sense I am there, because wherever you are, I am there too."

There were so many other questions Sabre might have asked his son about his new life, but they didn't matter. He was back with his son again and that was more important than any questions he might have had. Sabre was so pleased to hear that Theo was happy and at peace in his new world.

Sabre told Theo how angry he had been when he passed over and that his anger had made him hate everyone. He told Theo how he had used the gift of the Peace Pole the Supreme Life had given him, to spread fear and pain throughout the world. He had turned against everyone after losing his son. Tears ran down Sabre's face.

"Theo, I have been such a foolish man. I feel ashamed of the bad things I have done in my life and the hurt and pain I have caused," he sobbed. Theo hugged his father tight.

"The Supreme Life Force has forgiven you. He told me you were lost but now you're found. He loves and forgives you, Dad. Now you must forgive yourself."

Sabre wiped away his tears and made a vow to his son that when he returned back home, he would love, honour and serve the Supreme Life Force in his thoughts, words and actions for the rest of his life on Mother Earth.

"Dad, listen! Can you hear music?" Theo asked. The big bear pointed his ears in the direction of the forest. "Yes, Son, music and singing. There must be celebrations in the Magic Forest." "Let's join in the fun,"Theo said.

Father and son made their way down to a large clearing in the forest where they came across all the animals, birds and insects singing and dancing together.

Fatso the frog was first to welcome them and invite them to join in the birthday celebrations. The Magic Forest was five hundred years old that very day. Sabre picked his son up in his arms and started to dance around with him. He hugged his son close and kissed him on the forehead.

"I love you, Son," Sabre said with tears in his eyes. "I always will."
"Dad, you kept your promise. Together again! Remember you told me that before I passed over?"
"Yes, Son, I remember."

Sabre didn't want this day to end but just as the sun was setting Babakoochi appeared beside them. "I am sorry my friends, but it is time for us to leave the Magic Forest." He stepped back and let father and son say their goodbyes but both knew for sure that one day they would be back together again and then there would be no more goodbyes.

Sabre and Theo kissed and hugged each other, then Sabre signalled to Babakoochi that he was ready to leave. Theo and Babakoochi embraced and said it was good to finally meet each other. Sabre gave his son one last kiss goodbye then walked with Babakoochi towards the rainbow gateway. Just before he entered the gateway Theo shouted to him.

"Dad, always remember the message from the pearl - 'Death is not the end of life. My spirit will never leave you.'

Sabre blew a kiss towards his son. Theo caught the kiss in his paw and placed it up against his heart.
"I love you, dad. Remember the promise - Together again!"
"Love you too, Theo." Sabre shouted back.

Then he and Babakoochi walked through the rainbow gateway back into Sabre's homeland.

The great white bear had returned a different bear. All the bitterness and hurt had left his heart. He thanked Babakoochi for taking him to see his son.

"It's the Supreme Life Force you must thank," the young bear said. "It was him that brought you and Theo back together again."
"So be it!" replied Sabre.

Then the two friends embraced…. Sabre went on his way to a life of peace and harmony and Babakoochi returned home to his family.

May peace prevail on Earth.

The End

SUMMARY

So what have we learned from our little magic friend?

Although all seemed lost, it turned good at the end.

Talking, and swimming, silver pearls and honey bee's.

Honey popsticks, waterfalls, swinging from the trees.

We might not all know a little bear who brings magic, peace and love.

But remember that there's a power who lives somewhere up above.

If someone that you love, like Theo, has gone to a place that's far away.

With faith, hope and a little magic, you'll see them again some day.

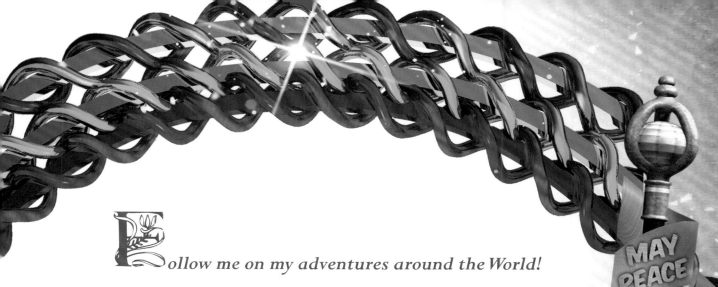

Follow me on my adventures around the World!

www.babakoochibear.com

https://www.facebook.com/Babakoochi

https://twitter.com/babakoochibear

MAY PEACE PREVAIL ON EARTH